PUFFIN BOOKS

Septimouse, Big Cheese!

Ann Jungman was born in London in 1938, the daughter of German-Jewish refugees. While studying Law she did some supply teaching at an all-girls' school. Ann decided to give up Law and did one year of post-graduate teacher training. She then spent a year in Israel, first working on a kibbutz and later as a secretary in Tel Aviv. She taught for six years in a variety of Inner London schools, before stopping to do an MA in American Studies, Literature and Comparative Education at London University.

Ann had always written stories for children while teaching, many of them about dragons and ghosts, princesses and vampires. In 1982, after many rejections and many years, *Vlad the Drac* was finally accepted by a small publisher. Its popularity and success enabled Ann finally to settle down and write full time. She spent many years in Australia, but now lives in London.

Septimouse, Big Cheese!

Ann Jungman

Illustrated by
Valeria Petrone

PUFFIN BOOKS

To Sam, with love

PUFFIN BOOKS

Published by the Penguin Group
Penguin Books Ltd, 27 Wrights Lane, London W8 5TZ, England
Penguin Books USA Inc., 375 Hudson Street, New York, New York 10014, USA
Penguin Books Australia Ltd, Ringwood, Victoria, Australia
Penguin Books Canada Ltd, 10 Alcorn Avenue, Toronto, Ontario, Canada M4V 3B2
Penguin Books (NZ) Ltd, 182–190 Wairau Road, Auckland 10, New Zealand

Penguin Books Ltd, Registered Offices: Harmondsworth, Middlesex, England

First published by Viking 1994
Published in Puffin Books 1995
3 5 7 9 10 8 6 4 2

Text copyright © Ann Jungman, 1994
Illustrations copyright © Valeria Petrone, 1994
All rights reserved

The moral right of the author has been asserted

Made and printed in Great Britain by Clays Ltd, St Ives plc

Contents

1

Septimouse to the Rescue

Septimouse stretched and yawned and fell back to sleep. He smiled as he slept, thinking happily what an exceptionally clever mouse he was.

"I am so wonderful," he muttered dreamily to himself. "What we seventh sons of seventh sons can do with our magical powers! I myself have built a mouse cheese factory so that all the mice in the neighbourhood have a regular and safe supply of delicious cheese. The local mice need no longer risk the big people's traps and it is all thanks to me. Yes, I have done very well and I deserve a good, long sleep."

But what Septimouse didn't know was

that his cheese factory was in danger! While Septimouse was having sweet dreams, his human friend, little big person Katie, was crying in her bedroom. Oscar the cat snuggled up to Katie, but she just carried on crying.

"This is serious," thought Oscar. "I'd better go and tell Septimouse, who, being the seventh son of a seventh son and having magical powers, will know what to do. Well, even if he *doesn't* know what to do, at least he will be able to talk to her and find out what is wrong."

So Oscar trotted downstairs, stood outside the mouse hole and called out, "Septi, old boy, miaow! Little big person Katie is crying and crying. You'd better come and talk to her."

Septimouse instantly woke up and raced out, and leapt on to Oscar's back.

"Quick!" he cried. "Take me to her!

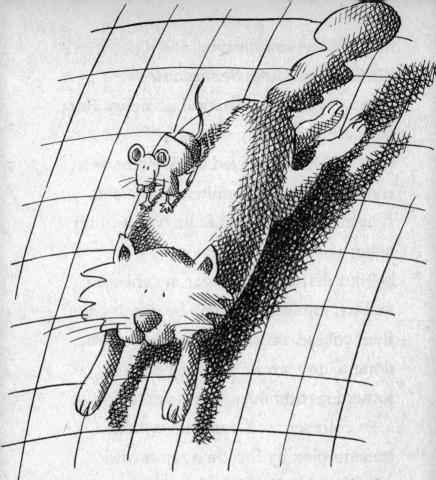

Not a moment to be lost!" Oscar rushed
upstairs and raced in through Katie's
door. She lay on her bed with her face
buried in a pillow, sobbing her heart out.

"Little big person Katie, what is this all
about? Now stop crying and tell me."

"Dad has lost his job."

"Oh dear," said Septimouse sympathetically. "That is bad news. But why are you crying so much?"

"Cos Mum and Dad say we'll have to move. We won't be able to afford this house any more." And she began to cry again.

"But that will endanger my cheese factory, and the mice will be deprived of their cheese. Something will have to be done. Don't worry, little big person Katie, I, Septimouse, the seventh son of a seventh son, will come up with a brilliant plan by this time tomorrow."

Katie sniffed and dried her eyes.

"Oh, I hope you do, Septimouse."

"I will, never fear, I most certainly will."

All that night Septimouse sat up reading *The Cheesemaker's Monthly*. Katie always bought the magazine for

Septimouse and he would use his
magical powers to shrink it and carry it
through to the mouse hole. He was
reading through the July issue, when
suddenly he leapt in the air and yelled.

"I've got it! I'm brilliant – it will work,
I'm sure it will, and we won't have to
lose our factory or our friend Oscar, or
little big person Katie."

In the morning Septimouse raced out
to tell Katie.

"She's not here," Oscar told him. "She's gone to some funny place where all the little big people go every day except Saturday and Sunday."

"Oh," said Septimouse. "That would be the place they call school. Very odd habit, I've always thought."

"Have you got a plan, Septi, old boy?" asked Oscar. "I don't want to move."

"I have indeed got a plan, Oscar – brilliant in its simplicity. We will not have to move, dear friend, never fear."

Oscar and Septimouse waited by the door for Katie to arrive home from school. Katie came in with her mother; Septimouse quickly hid.

"Miaow," said Oscar loudly, staring hard at Katie.

"I'm going upstairs, Mum," she said. "I'll take Oscar."

As she bent to pick up the cat,

Septimouse jumped up and down and
waved. Quickly she grabbed him,
popped him in her pocket and raced
upstairs. She dived into her room and
pulled Septimouse out of her pocket and
put him on her bed.

"Little big person, I, Septimouse the Great, have come up with a brilliant solution to your problem."

"What is it? Please tell me, Septimouse."

"Big, big person Dad must set up a cheese factory and make cheese, just the way we do in my mouse factory."

"Would that make money?" asked Katie.

"I am led to believe it would," the mouse told her. "For in *The Cheesemaker's Monthly* I read that English cheeses are getting more and more popular, that there are always new cheeses being launched and that there is a market for them."

"I wonder if Dad would be interested in your idea," mused Katie.

"You must arrange for me to talk to him."

"He'll think it's odd. I mean, he's never met a talking mouse before."

"Neither had you, and now we're the best of friends. Let me stay in your pocket and I'll pick a good time to talk to him."

That night they were eating supper. Dad picked at his food miserably.

"I went to see the estate agent today. He's going to put a *For Sale* notice up tomorrow."

"No way, sir!" cried Septimouse. "That will not be necessary."

Mum and Dad looked around to see where the voice was coming from. Katie took Septimouse out of her pocket and stood him on the table.

"Look no further, big, big person Dad and big, big person Mum, it is I, Septimouse the Great, the seventh son of

a seventh son, and your humble tenant,
who speaks."

Mum and Dad stared at the smiling
mouse in amazement.

"Septimouse lives with his family in
the mouse hole over there by the fridge,"
Katie explained. "He has magic powers
and can speak on account of being a 4S."

"A 4S?" asked her mother weakly.

"Yes," said Septimouse. "It's a short
version of the seventh son of a seventh

son. Now, as your house and daughter have been so very helpful to me in setting up my cheese factory, I want to help you in this difficult time."

"Help us? How?"

"By showing you how to start your own cheese factory, so that you can get rich and stay in this house for ever."

"You really have a cheese factory in this house?" asked Mum, amazed.

"I most certainly do, and you and big, big person Dad are coming to see how wonderful it is with your very own eyes." And, holding up his arms, he sang:

"Big, big people in a trice,
Be as small as little mice."

A second later a miniature Mum and Dad were sitting on their huge chairs.

Katie picked them up and carried them over to the mouse hole.

"Welcome to my magnificent mouse cheese factory," said Septimouse. "Please step inside."

Mum and Dad were shown round by Mr Mouse and then had a cheese-tasting session with all the mice.

"Delicious!" said Dad.

"Wonderful!" said Mum.

"Yes, and as you can see," said Septimouse, "very easy to make when you know how. Here is the recipe. When I make you into big, big people again the recipe will grow with you. Now, let me return you to your home. Any time you need to consult me about anything, just tell little big person Katie. She knows how to get in touch with me."

Soon Mum and Dad were their usual size. Dad studied the recipe.

"It really doesn't seem difficult or expensive to make," he commented. "And it *is* delicious."

"Are you going to give it a try?" asked Katie eagerly.

"Why not?" said her father, smiling. "If Septimouse can do it, so can I!"

2

Finding the Factory

The very next day, Dad and Mum sat down with Septimouse to discuss what should be done next.

"Perhaps you could suggest something, Septimouse," said Mum, "since neither big, big person Dad nor I know anything about making cheese."

"It's not difficult," Septimouse assured her. "But I feel it is important to have the right premises. Your house is quite excellent for us mice, but I think it would be too small to make people's cheeses as well."

"Oh, definitely," agreed Dad. "I'll go into the estate agent tomorrow and get some information about commercial premises."

"What are commercial premises?" asked Septimouse.

"Places where people work rather than live," Katie explained.

"I see," said Septimouse. "So you will continue to live here, but will make the cheese on these 'commercial premises'?"

"Exactly," replied Mum. "But we can only stay here if we make a success of the cheese factory. We will all have to work very hard."

"Madam," declared Septimouse, "have no doubt that this venture will succeed, since *my* home as well as yours is at stake. In fact, not only my home, but my business too. Yes, definitely – the People's 4S Cheese Factory must take off."

"What do you mean, 4S cheese?" inquired Dad.

"My cheese is called 4S cheese, after me, on account of me being the seventh son of a seventh son."

"We would have to think of another reason for calling it 4S cheese for people," said Katie. "I mean, if we said it was called after a mouse who was the seventh son of a seventh son, everyone would think we were nuts."

"Think of words beginning with 's' that describe cheese," said Septimouse.

"Super," said Dad.

"Smashing," said Katie.

"Scrumptious," added the mouse.

"You've used up all the words," groaned Mum. "I can't think of another one."

"Go on, try," chorused the others.

"Salivating," declared Mum, smiling.

"What does *that* mean?" asked Septimouse.

"It means mouth-watering," explained Dad.

"Oh well, my cheese *is* definitely mouth-watering," declared the mouse. "Yes, that will do very well for the fourth word. So your 4S cheese is a Super, Smashing, Scrumptious, Salivating cheese. Yes, that should sell it very well."

"That's all well and good," said Dad, "but we haven't got anywhere to make our 4S cheese yet. We need to start looking for our commercial premises straight away. No time to be lost."

"I'd better come with you," said Septimouse. "I know more about making cheese than you, so I should help choose the premises."

So the next week Dad put Septimouse in his pocket and went off to look at places to let.

As they went into the first place on the list, Septimouse stuck his head out of Dad's pocket. "Looks all right from the outside," he declared.

"Just wait till you see the inside," said the estate agent, smiling.

"What?" asked Dad, slightly puzzled.

"You said that you thought the outside looked all right," said the estate agent.

"No I didn't," replied Dad. "I haven't said a word."

"Must be hearing things," muttered the estate agent. "Well, let's go in anyway."

They went in and the estate agent put on the lights.

"What did you say your new business was going to be, sir?" he asked.

"Er . . . cheese," said Dad. "I am going to make a new brand of cheese."

"A new brand of cheese?" complained Septimouse. "*The* new brand of cheese!"

That time Dad heard Septimouse and pushed the mouse back into his pocket.

"Sorry," he said to the estate agent. "I

used to be a ventriloquist, and when I'm worried I sort of carry on conversations with myself."

"I see," sniffed the estate agent. "Well, what do you think of the premises, sir? They are very light and airy, just the thing for a large dairy, I would have thought."

"A large dairy?" declared Septimouse. "Not a dairy, a *cheese factory*!"

Once again Dad pushed Septimouse down.

"There I go again," he laughed. "Arguing with myself – my wife and daughter are always teasing me about it."

"I can imagine, sir. Now what exactly do you need for your . . . um . . . cheese factory?"

"You know, now that I am here, I realize I haven't thought this thing

through at all. I need to think about it.
Maybe I should go and look at some
other cheese factories and make notes,
and then come back to you."

"Good thinking, big, big person Dad,"
commented Septimouse.

Dad laughed nervously. "There I go
again – I feel so foolish. Well, thanks for
showing me round. I'll get back to you
when I've had a chance to look at other
places and take some measurements and
things. Bye." And Dad ran out of the

building and jumped into the car. He sat
in the driver's seat and wiped his
forehead.

"That was one of the worst
experiences I ever had," Dad told
Septimouse. "I'm lucky the man didn't
run away. I am never going to take you
out with me again."

"Hum," said Septimouse. "Well, I'm
sorry I embarrassed you, but, come to
think of it, my father, the excellent Mr

Mouse, knows more about premises than I do. Let us ask him to go with you next time. He can't speak. There will be no trouble there. He can look at the different premises and report back to me and then you and I can compare notes and decide which of the many buildings at our disposal should have the honour of housing our 4S cheese factory."

So on the next visits Mr Mouse went with Dad to look at premises and apart from a few quiet squeaks was suitably silent and still. When they got back Mr Mouse told Septimouse what he thought of the different places they had seen. Dad and Mr Mouse were in complete agreement, and a building quite near the house was decided upon.

3

Growing

"Quiet!" shouted Septimouse, banging on the table. "Quiet! I call this meeting to order. Now, those present at this extraordinary meeting, called to discuss turning the new premises into a 4S cheese factory, are big, big person Dad, big, big person Mum, little big person Katie, Mr Mouse, and the chairmouse is myself, Septimouse the Great. Big, big person Dad, I believe you have something to say on the matter?"

"Well, only that, as you all know, we have found suitable premises and now we need to convert them into a cheese factory. Where do you think we should start?" said Dad.

Mr Mouse stood up on the table and squeaked excitedly at Septimouse, who nodded and made notes. Mum and Dad and Katie sat and stared. After a while Mr Mouse stopped squeaking and went back to his place.

"My honoured father says," Septimouse began, "that he has already built one cheese factory and has no doubt that he can build another one, but that the scale of this operation might . . . "

"Septimouse," interrupted Katie, "this is going to take for ever. If you *are* such a special mouse, couldn't you use your 4S powers to give your father the power of human speech?"

"That, little big person Katie, is an excellent idea. I shall have to consult with my honoured father and see what he feels about it."

The two mice squeaked at each other for a little while, then Septimouse raised his front paws in the air and intoned:

"Honoured Father, Mr Mouse,
We are in need of your nous,
Like a human you shall speak,
No longer with a mousie squeak."

They all looked at Mr Mouse, who looked embarrassed.

"Well," he said, "I don't know what you lot expect me to say."

And he giggled and hid his face.

Mum and Dad looked at each other with relief. At least Mr Mouse spoke plain English.

"It worked!" shrieked Katie. "Septimouse, you've done it again. You are wonderful."

"I know," agreed Septimouse. "Now,

come on, little big person. No time to waste. Singing my praises doesn't get one single cheese made. Honoured Father, how can we launch our venture on the world with all possible speed?"

"I can only speak from my experience with our mouse cheese factory," said Mr

Mouse, "but a lot of work needs to be done. We will have to put heating in and keep the temperature even at all times. Then we need vats to make the cheese."

"Yes," said Dad. "And we will need fridges to store the milk and to keep the cheeses in after they are made."

"And we will have to wrap the cheese and put a 4S stamp on it before we take it round to the shops," added Mum.

"And we will have to get vans to deliver the cheese," chipped in Katie.

"I can see this is going to be a very big operation," said Mr Mouse, shaking his head. "It will be far more complicated than our mouse cheese factory. You see, we just made the cheese and then ate it ourselves or gave it to other mice who came to the mouse hole. Yes, this will be more difficult. Now let me see, we will need . . ."

Soon Mr Mouse had made a long list of what was needed and handed it to Dad.

"Can you work out what all this will cost," Mr Mouse asked, "in that funny stuff you big, big people call money?"

"Give it to me," said Mum. "I'm good at that."

So Mum worked it all out, then Mr Mouse said they would need at least seven people to work long hours on the site to get the factory ready quickly.

"I don't see how we can afford to pay seven sets of wages," Mum told them, shaking her head. "We'll use up all our savings just buying the materials that we'll need."

"I knew we'd bitten off more than we could chew," groaned Dad.

"Can't you get some more money?" asked Septimouse.

"No way," answered Dad. "Not now that I'm going to be unemployed."

"I've got it!" yelled Katie. "Septimouse, you're not the only genius around here. Your father and brothers know how to build a cheese factory. Why not use them?"

"Because, little big person Katie, they are too small by far."

"Not if you used your great magical powers to make them as big as people."

"Now that *is* a good idea," agreed

Septimouse. "I can't imagine why I
didn't think of it myself. That is what we
shall do. My father and brothers will
help you build the factory. Yes, this is all
working out very well indeed."

4

A Problem

"Come on, everyone," Dad called into the mouse hole. "I'm ready to go."

"Coming, big, big person Dad," replied Septimouse. "My honoured mother, Mrs Mouse, is just making our lunch, and she isn't quite finished. She sends her apologies. My mother wants to come with us to see that none of us overwork and that we all eat enough."

"Right," said Dad. "I've got a nice comfortable basket for you all to travel in, so ready when you are."

The mice trooped out, and Dad picked them up and put them into the basket. Mrs Mouse carried her own tiny basket with all the lunches neatly folded inside it.

"I hope you're in good form today," Dad told Septimouse as he put him in the basket. "You're going to have to make the bread and cheese grow, as well as the mice."

"Don't tell me," groaned Septimouse. "But fear not, big, big person Dad, my magic will not fail you, for am I not the seventh son of a seventh son?"

Dad picked the mouse up, placed him in the basket and closed the lid. He was carrying the basket to the door, when he tripped over Oscar, and fell.

"You stupid cat," snapped Dad. "Whatever are you doing?"

Oscar looked at him and started to miaow.

Septimouse stuck his head out of the basket.

"Excuse me, big, big person Dad, but Oscar is saying that he doesn't want to be left behind on his own. He wants to come to the premises too."

Dad groaned. "Why?"

"Well, he feels that his cream is going to be made there and he wants to see that all goes well."

"He can't come," said Dad crossly. "There won't be room in the car for all the tools and your basket and the cat basket as well."

"Miaow," said Septimouse to Oscar.

"Miaow, miaow, miaowww!" replied Oscar, giving Dad a dirty look.

"Oscar says that he will travel with us and I must shrink him," Septimouse said.

"Oh, all right," sniffed Dad. "Get on with it then."

Septimouse stood on the edge of the basket and closed his eyes.

"Oscar, friend to every mouse,
Shrink so you can enter this house –
    well, basket."

41

A moment later a tiny Oscar gave a
tiny "miaow", which was his way of
saying "thank you", and climbed into
the basket and curled up with the mice.

When they arrived at the factory, Dad
carried the basket in and opened it up
and the mice and Oscar clambered out.

"Right," commanded Septimouse.
"John, James, Julius, Joseph, Jeremy,
Jack and Honoured Mother and
Honoured Father, please stand in a line,

for I am about to make some very powerful magic, of the kind only available to the seventh son of a seventh son." And he closed his eyes tightly and held his hands up in the air.

"Eight mice in a row,
People-sized you must grow."

Dad gasped as he looked at eight mice as big as himself.

"You did it, Septimouse. Oh, well done!"

Septimouse yawned. "Nothing to it, big, big person Dad, nothing at all – for the seventh son of a seventh son, that is."

"Miaow!" said Oscar plaintively, "Miaow. Septi, old boy, why are those other mice so big? I'm not sure I like it."

"Nothing to worry about, Oscar,"

Septimouse explained. "My father and brothers are going to build a people-sized factory, so it is better if they are people-sized."

"Oh," muttered the cat. "Well, if you say so, Septi, but I prefer mice to be smaller than me."

"Let's get on," insisted Dad, "or the whole day will have gone. Septimouse, please explain to your father and brothers that we want the vats over in this corner, and the pipes will have to go along this wall, and . . . "

"No need to bother, big, big person Dad. My father and brothers will know what to do. All they need is the plan. Just put it down here and I will tell them what it says."

"In that case, what is there for me to do?" asked Dad.

"Nothing really. You're not needed,"

Septimouse replied.

Mrs Mouse made a loud squeaking sound and looked at Dad. All the other mice looked at him too, and laughed.

"What's going on, Septimouse?" asked Dad, feeling a bit uncomfortable.

"My honoured mother wants to help with the building, now that she is people-sized, and she suggests that you can start to make lunch for everyone. She says she is bored with food and wants to learn some new skills."

"Oh well," said Dad. "I'll be in charge of food then."

So while the eight mice set about painting the walls and carrying wood and nailing things together and digging trenches for pipes, Dad made them all a cup of tea.

"I wasn't sure what they'd want to drink," he told Septimouse. "I can heat up some milk if the tea isn't right." But the mice enjoyed the tea and then went straight back to work.

By lunch-time they were all exhausted and very hungry. Dad took them two rounds of cheese sandwiches each and more tea and some Jaffa Cakes.

"My sandwiches!" cried Mrs Mouse. "They are mouse-sized. They won't do at all! Septimouse, my son, maybe you should make us into our own size again."

"Yes," shouted his brothers, "and quickly. We're starving!"

"That will not be necessary," replied Septimouse, and he raised his hands up above his head and muttered at the sandwiches.

A moment later the sandwiches grew to human size.

"Well done, Septimouse!" cried the

mice, and they tucked in greedily.

"See," said Septimouse. "Easy as falling off a log. Not a single problem."

"Touch wood," said Dad nervously.

At that moment they heard a scream and looked up to see some schoolchildren staring through the window in horror.

"Don't be scared," shouted Dad, "I can explain everything."

"Little big people, come back, come back this instant!" called Septimouse. "I, Septimouse, the seventh son of a seventh son, command it."

But the children ran away in terror.

"Now we're in trouble," groaned Dad. "As easy as falling off a log indeed!"

"What should we do?" asked Mr Mouse nervously.

"I think we should get out of here as soon as possible," said Dad. "Come on,

Septimouse, get shrinking. We don't want people asking questions."

"Oh dear," sighed Septimouse. "The best-laid plans of mice and men are liable to go wrong now and again. Honoured Father, Honoured Mother and brothers, and Oscar the cat, please line up."

The mice dutifully lined up in a row.

"Eight mice (and Oscar) in a row,
To your own size you must go."

The mice and cat instantly shrank.

"Into the basket quickly," commanded Dad, and the mice jumped in as fast as they could. Mrs Mouse gave a squeak.

"Honoured Mother wants her basket," Septimouse told Dad. Dad grabbed it and threw it into the bigger basket. Just then they heard a screech of brakes, and four policemen jumped out of a car outside.

Dad groaned and picked up the basket.

"Good afternoon, sir," said one of the policemen, appearing in the doorway. "We are just checking on a very odd rumour. Some kids said they saw giant mice here, eating sandwiches."

Dad roared with nervous laughter. "Nothing like that, officer. My workmen were having lunch and some of them put on silly masks. Now they have taken the afternoon off."

"I knew it must be something like that," replied the policeman. "Sorry to bother you, sir."

"No problem," smiled Dad. "I'll just lock up and I'll be off too." And he breathed a huge sigh of relief as the police car drove off.

5

The Solution

Dad arrived home and put the basket down near the mouse hole. Then he slumped at the kitchen table, his head buried in his hands.

"Whatever happened?" asked Mum sympathetically, as she put the kettle on.

"I don't want to talk about it," moaned Dad, "but I think we will have to forget all about the cheese factory."

"We can't forget about it!" cried Mum. "We've sunk all our savings into it – every penny."

Katie came in from school, just in time to hear what Mum said.

"Dad!" she cried. "Whatever happened?"

Her father just shook his head and looked despairing.

Katie went over to the mouse hole and called, "Septimouse, it is I, little big person Katie. Could you come out and explain to big, big person Mum and me why big, big person Dad is so upset?"

Septimouse ran out immediately. "Little big person Katie, it all went wrong. Even I, Septimouse, could not prevent the disaster. I suffered a public defeat, everyone saw it – my mother and father, big, big person Dad, all my six brothers *and* Oscar. I am humiliated, little big person, and I do not wish to communicate with anyone."

"Please, Septimouse, please, please, *please* just tell big, big person Mum and me what happened, then we will leave you to recover from your defeat in peace."

"If you insist, little big person, but I feel very sad and heavy inside, not like myself at all. Maybe my special powers have deserted me."

"You're still talking to me, Septimouse," Katie pointed out. "You can still speak like big, big and little big people."

"Ah, that is true, little big person Katie, thank you for pointing that out. Yes, indeed. Maybe our defeat was just temporary. Put me on the table, please."

Katie put him on the table and
Septimouse related the events of the day,
not leaving out a single detail, while Dad
groaned at the description of each
episode.

"Oh dear," said Mum. "I see. So we
can't use the mice as labour and we can't
afford to pay anyone else."

"And we've spent all our money on
materials," added Dad. "I blame myself.
I should never have listened to a
mouse."

"Sorry," said Septimouse miserably.

"It's not your fault," said Dad, feeling a bit guilty. "You couldn't be expected to know anything about cheese-making for people."

"I was trying to help, big, big person Dad," sniffed Septimouse in a small voice.

"Stop it, you two," cried Katie. "You are giving up much too easily. I have had the most wonderful idea."

All eyes turned on Katie.

"You said that Mrs Mouse made cheese sandwiches for all the mice, didn't you?"

"Yes," agreed Dad. "So what of it?"

"What of it? What's the matter with you all? Don't you see? If Septimouse can make the sandwiches grow, he can make the mice cheeses grow too. We won't need a factory. The cheese can be made here and then Septimouse can do his seventh son of a seventh son magic on them and make them people-sized."

"Oh, little big person Katie, I love you. You have made me feel like Septimouse the Great again!"

"Do you think you can do it?" asked Dad.

"Pray do not try the patience of the Great Septimouse with such foolish questions," replied the mouse, puffing himself up.

"Let's try it," suggested Mum. "You go and get a cheese, Septimouse, and let's give it a try."

So Katie put Septimouse down by the mouse hole and a few moments later Mr Mouse rolled a cheese out of the hole and into the kitchen.

"Well, go on, Septimouse," said Dad. "Don't leave us in suspense."

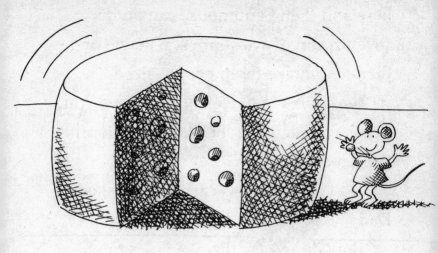

Septimouse, watched by all the mice
and Mum and Dad and Katie, put his
arm up over the cheese and intoned:

"Mouse cheese, you are small,
We need you bigger for us all.
Grow, grow to people size,
Let everyone know I am still wise."

They all held their breath. The cheese
grew and grew. Dad picked it up and

danced with it. The mice all cheered.
Mum and Katie hugged each other.

Then Dad put the cheese on the table
and cut a slice. He gave a bit to Mum, a
bit to Katie and a smaller bit to
Septimouse.

Very seriously they all took a bite.

"Delicious!" yelled Mum.

"Scrumptious!" shouted Katie.

"Magnificent!" shrieked Dad. "We

won't need a factory. All we need is you mice, and Septimouse to work magic, and we will all be rich. Septimouse, you're wonderful. Forgive me my moment of doubt."

"You are forgiven, big, big person Dad. You are not familiar with the ways of seventh sons of seventh sons, but you will learn, as I should have remembered, that we are never wrong and never defeated."

After that there were few problems. The mice made more cheese, and when they felt tired Septimouse would shrink Mum and Dad and Katie and they would go and work a shift.

The cheese factory premises were turned into a storage space full of refrigerators and Mum had a van marked "4S Cheeses" to make deliveries. She went to all the shops that sold cheeses to try to persuade them to take some 4S cheese and had a lot of success.

Soon many shops carried the new line of cheese and the orders began to come in fast and furious. The mice worked very hard and all seemed to be well . . . until the phone rang one day. Mum answered it.

"Yes, that is right, this is 4S Cheese Manufacturers here. Oh, well yes, I suppose so. You'd better speak to the manager. It's the Environmental Health people," she whispered to Dad. "They want to come and inspect the factory where we make the cheese."

"Oh no!" groaned Dad. "This is the end, this is really the end. Now we are in the most terrible trouble. We won't be able to conceal the fact that our 4S cheese is made by mice."

6
Solved!

Mum and Dad stared at each other in horror. Mum sighed deeply and whispered to Dad, "We'll have to agree to let them come."

"I know," agreed Dad. "But goodness knows what will happen when they find out that we've been marketing cheese made by mice."

"Well," commented Mum, "we are about to find out. I suppose they will fine us or put us in prison."

"One thing is for sure. They'll definitely close us down," said Dad. "And we'll have to sell the house after all."

"I think we should put this inspection

off as long as possible. Maybe
Septimouse will have one of his brilliant
4S ideas to get us off the hook and by the
time the inspector turns up everything
will be sorted out," said Mum hopefully.

"I doubt it. I think this situation will be
too much even for Septimouse, 4S or no
4S," groaned Dad. "But give me the
phone. I'd better talk to them. Here we

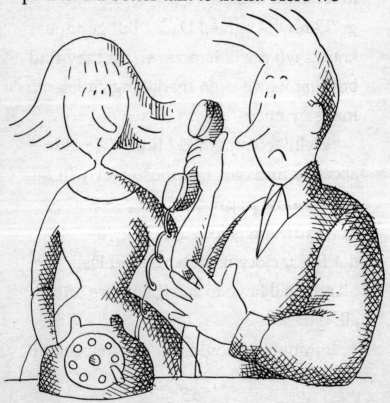

go, 'We who are about to die salute you,' as the gladiators used to say. Good morning. This is the manager of 4S Cheeses Incorporated. I understand you wish to inspect our premises. No, there is no problem. It's just that we are very busy. Would next week suit you? Friday afternoon? Yes, splendid. I will look forward to meeting you. Thank you, good bye."

Dad put the phone down and they both rushed over to the mouse hole and knelt down.

"Septimouse," called Mum, "could you come out please? We've got an unexpected crisis on our hands and we need your help."

"The factory is in danger again," added Dad.

Septimouse stuck his head out of the hole, yawning.

"Big, big person Mum and big, big person Dad, I was asleep. Whatever has happened can't be that serious."

"It is," Mum told him. "It really is. An inspector is coming to make a check on the cheese-making premises."

"That's not a problem," replied Septimouse. "Our cheese factory is immaculate. It would pass any test a big, big person chose to devise."

"But, Septimouse," protested Dad, "you don't understand. This inspector can't know that you and your family make the cheese. It would cause the most terrible outcry."

"I don't see why," sniffed Septimouse. "If I, with my amazing 4S powers, can create a cheese that big, big people enjoy eating, why should some inspector person object? Now, when is this big, big person inspector coming? I will see to it

that our factory is scrubbed and the
inspector person will not find a single
thing to object to."

"Septimouse, you don't mean you will
shrink the inspector?"

"Well, of course I will shrink the
inspector. How else could one of you
huge, outsized big, big people see how
we make cheese down here? Now, I
want to go back to sleep. Please tell me
when the inspection will take place. I will

put it in my diary and tell my honoured family to expect the visit."

"It's next Friday, at three o'clock," said Mum faintly.

"That is all I need to know," commented the mouse. "Now I shall return to my mouse hole and you can stop worrying. Everything will be absolutely fine. I have no doubt that the inspector will be very impressed by our cheese, our factory and of course, last but not least, by me. Big, big person Mum and big, big person Dad, I wish you a very good afternoon. Now I wish to sleep. Please don't disturb me again."

When Katie came home from school her parents told her what had happened.

Katie giggled. "That inspector is going to get the shock of her life, isn't she?"

"You don't think we should let Septimouse shrink the inspector, do you?'' demanded Mum.

"Well, I don't see what else we can do," replied Katie. "I mean, that is how the cheese is made and there isn't any time to build another factory. You know what Septimouse is like. He always manages to sort things out, being the seventh son of a seventh son and all that. And it is true that the mouse cheese factory is very clean indeed. I bet it's cleaner than most human cheese dairies.

I don't think we should worry. I bet she will love Septimouse and will be very intrigued by the way the mouse cheese is made. I mean, it must be very boring to be an inspector. This will be a real change for her."

"I'm not so optimistic," sniffed her father.

"You mustn't let her go till I come home from school," grinned Katie. "I can't wait to hear how she feels about it."

"I just hope you and Septimouse are right," said her mother, "because if you're not we are going to be in a real mess."

7

The Final Test

On the Friday, at exactly 3 p.m., the front doorbell rang. Dad went to answer the door, while Mum and Septimouse waited in the kitchen.

"Would you come into the kitchen, please," said Dad.

"The kitchen!" exclaimed the inspector. "I thought I was going to be shown round a factory, not a private house."

"And so you are, madam," cried Septimouse. "And not any old factory, but my very own 4S cheese factory."

The inspector stared at Septimouse and then at Mum and Dad.

"It's a mouse and it can talk," she

said. "What's going on here?"

"Madam, do not alarm yourself. Let me introduce myself. I am Septimouse, the seventh son of a seventh son, and I have magical powers, including the capacity for human speech."

"How extraordinary!" gasped the inspector, sitting down and staring at Septimouse.

"Yes, indeed, Big, Big Person Madam Inspector, I am most extraordinary – quite wonderful in fact. Now, let me explain about my cheese factory."

"*Your* cheese factory?"

"Yes, madam. I, Septimouse, have a cheese factory in the mouse hole you can see over there next to the fridge. That place, madam, is where the 4S cheese, enjoyed by all who taste it, is created."

"It's not possible," declared the inspector, shaking her head. "For one thing, the cheeses are too big."

"Anticipating that very objection, Madam Big, Big Person Inspector, I have a mouse-sized cheese here before me. Now, watch carefully. Something very amazing is about to happen before your

71

very eyes." And Septimouse intoned:

"Mouse cheese, you are small,
We need you bigger for us all.
Grow, grow to people size,
Let everyone know that I am wise."

As the cheese grew the inspector's mouth fell open.

"Big, Big Person Inspector, please try a morsel," said Septimouse.

The astonished inspector took a slice, nibbled at it and then burst into a smile. "It's delicious," she declared. "Very special indeed."

"Of course," agreed Septimouse.

"The only problem is that I won't be able to inspect the premises," commented the inspector, "to give you people a clean bill of health."

"Oh, but you can," Mum assured her. "Septimouse can expand and shrink people as well as cheeses. He often shrinks us and we go down and work in the cheese factory."

"Shrink me?" said the inspector. "Are you serious?"

"Most definitely we are," cried the mouse, holding up his hands.

"Big, big person in a trice,
Be as small as little mice."

And there was the shrunken inspector sitting on her chair looking very surprised.

"Don't worry," Mum told her. "It's fun. I'll carry you over to the mouse hole, and then Septimouse will take over."

Gently Mum put the inspector down by the mouse hole.

Septimouse took her by the hand, they waved to Mum and Dad and went into the cheese factory.

Katie rushed into the house, from school.

"Where's the inspector?" she asked.

Mum and Dad pointed to the hole and the three of them sat at the kitchen table and waited anxiously. After a while the inspector and Septimouse came out together, laughing. Mum, Dad and Katie breathed a sigh of relief. Mum picked the

inspector up in one hand and
Septimouse in the other and put them on
the table.

"It was wonderful," said the inspector.
"I never saw a cleaner factory and it was
such fun. I'm not at all used to work
being fun."

"Everything should be fun, madam,"
cried Septimouse. "We mice organize
things much better than you big, big

people. We enjoy every aspect of our lives. Now, before I make you big, big person-sized again, I want you to promise to come and visit us often. My honoured mother will be very hurt if you don't."

"I promise," agreed the inspector, smiling.

Septimouse held up his hands and cried:

> "Shrunken person become large,
> This I say and I'm in charge."

Suddenly there was a full-sized inspector standing on the kitchen table, looking a bit foolish.

"Well," said the inspector, as she climbed down, "what an extraordinary day. I shall have to come back every week to see my new mouse friends, as I promised."

"You're not going to report us then?" asked Dad.

"Nothing to report," the inspector assured him. "I never saw a more hygienic workplace. The fact that the workers are mice is really neither here nor there – no one's business, in fact."

"We can go on making cheese?" asked Katie.

"I should be very angry if you didn't," said the inspector.

So cheeses poured out of the house and

into the shops. A year later every cheese counter in Britain carried a wonderful new English cheese called 4S, which tasted like no other cheese anyone had ever tasted. One evening Septimouse was invited to dinner with Katie and her parents. After dinner he showed them an article in *The Cheesemaker's Monthly*.

"They say my cheese has been awarded the 'Cheese of the Year' award," Septimouse told them, his chest swelling with pride. "So you definitely won't have to move."

"No, and it is all thanks to you. Is there any way at all we can repay you, Septimouse?"

"There is only one thing I would really like," Septimouse told them, "and that is to see my cheese in a shop. Would you take me to a shop just once, please?"

So Mum and Dad and Katie set off for

the local supermarket, with Septimouse
hidden in Katie's pocket. The mouse
kept peeping out and looking at all the
food.

"Oh me, oh my," he said repeatedly as
they passed counter upon counter of
food.

When they came to the cheese counter,
Septimouse looked at the huge array of
cheeses.

"Oh me, oh my, a mouse paradise,"
he whispered.

Then he saw it! In the middle of the display was the biggest cheese you ever saw, with a big notice on it:

4S Cheese, the Cheese of the Year

"Oh me, oh my," cried Septimouse, "my cheese! Oh, this is the happiest moment of my life, little big person Katie. Septimouse the Great is finally recognized for the unique genius that he undoubtedly is."